AMOL BHAGWATI

Musical
MYSTICISM

BLUEROSE PUBLISHERS
India | U.K.

Copyright © Amol Bhagwati 2024

All rights reserved by author. No part of this publication may be reproduced, stored in a retrieval system or transmitted in any form or by any means, electronic, mechanical, photocopying, recording or otherwise, without the prior permission of the author. Although every precaution has been taken to verify the accuracy of the information contained herein, the publisher assumes no responsibility for any errors or omissions. No liability is assumed for damages that may result from the use of information contained within.

BlueRose Publishers takes no responsibility for any damages, losses, or liabilities that may arise from the use or misuse of the information, products, or services provided in this publication.

For permissions requests or inquiries regarding this publication,
please contact:

BLUEROSE PUBLISHERS
www.BlueRoseONE.com
info@bluerosepublishers.com
+91 8882 898 898
+4407342408967

ISBN: 978-93-6261-363-9

Cover design: Shivam
Typesetting: Namrata Saini

First Edition: August 2024

PREFACE

When musical notes and poetic verses suffuse, they create a melody of words and litany music. Intertwined music and verse emit the ecstasy or poignancy of the heart through verses running into spate (river of emotions running into spate) and overflowing abundance of music filling the space with melody, mirth and mellifluence. Words, meanings and melody are like the creator, preserver and re-creator in our Hindu pantheon for the primal source of energy triplicated in a purpose, designated to each trajectory for the larger benefit of civilization and culture.

Some melodies which are performed in concerts have the distinguished quality of being immemorial for the aesthetic experience provided. These have converted from soundscapes to word images.

From an auditory perspective to a visual one. Some visual images etched for beauty, serenity, serendipity have been transformed into images of verse to enliven the aesthetic experience. Some mythological poignant events and characters have created and inspiration which find a place in poetry.

Life is a transition of emotions ranging from ephemeral to almost eternal. The various shades of beauty alter into various forms and nuances in scorching sun, the frost bites, digits of the moon and transiting seasons which bring out the poignant and profuse in our beings. The blessings of love and seasons manifest into soft whisperings, concern, empathy and culminate like full bloom of the lotus flower where love and coexistence are always flowering in the hearts of lovers and poets.

With conviction, finesse and immersion of self, the most memorable form of art can be created. To quote the verses of John Keats

"A thing of beauty is a joy forever:

Its loveliness increases; it will never pass into nothingness; but will still will keep

A bower quite for us, and a sleep

Full of sweet dreams and health and quite breathing."

(Endymion, line 1)

Contents

Mythology 1

Beauty 15

Music 29

Nature 43

Rain 57

Mythology

Musical mysticism

As divinity unfolds, through reams of cloth.
Through words of wisdom, whispered and manifested,
Striking a chord in the expansive munificent horizon of the mind.
Beauty and beyond what it transpires and perceives,
Through the sinuous arrows of striking intent.
Through the shroud of mystic beyond the reverberation,
What is either in the nether or ether world and much beyond;
Within the reams of the mind.

Munificent- Magnanimous
Reverberation- Echo

Amol Bhagwati

Over the snowy Himalayas, the beauteous layers of pristine moon beams,
In the heart of Uma, pours out a dance of emotions.

Transformation of darkness into light,
Through aeons and immortal dance of destruction and creation.
In the locks of hair of Uma dance, the nascent moon which spreads,
Being moonlight as a layer of the profound knowledge of Shiva.

Excessive ecstasy through the cosmic dance of (Anand Tandav)
Shiva again re-establishes the fallen earing on his ear,
(Through the sway of his legs), as effortlessly as he creates new life.

Aeon- Yugas

Musical mysticism

The manifestation of the mind became momentous either logically or emotionally.
In the Kurukshetra of the life there is turmoil between selfishness and selflessness.

You are the Pandav, you are the Kaurav you are your own ultimate objective.

You have to gain victory over the self, what is nobler than that?
In the soul of Arjun, the egotism of Duryodhan strives,
you have to become Krishna for you self too.

The values and ethos are stripped like reams of cloth like thousand Dushans,
Sacrifice yourself at the end of an epoch and your aspirations and tribulations too.

Where power is blind like Dhritrashtra and helpless like Bhishm,
Where cowardice, plotting and avarice is a practice like that of Shakuni.

What do you gain after losing yourself in the game of dice?
Oh enlightened one?

Is the earth ever expanded by performing Rajsuya sacrifice?
In the anticipation of future and fond hopes one is pestle like Abhimanyu,
Where righteousness and principles are always living in secret exile.

At the end of eighteen days Armies of eighteen Akshauhani are crumbled to dust,
Do we call this life/s strife and struggle as Mahabharat?

Amol Bhagwati

What vanished with the Palace of Illusions was their fortitude,
What was strengthened in the twelve years?
Of exile the fraternity and cohesiveness?
The year of incognito unveiled their,
Covert desires in form of servitude,
And prepared the whole era for the end of an aeon,
Surreptitiously and serenaded to collision.
The Palace of Illusion eluded the Pandavas to their covert visions,
Fantasies and overt ambition,
Leading to the fateful game of dices,
Testing the potency of lethal poison loaded in the dice.
Where the Shree of their fortunes was staked,
After losing sanity one own freedom and entity,
What was lost what was won it never betrayed,
Aryavarta lost its magnificence resplendent,
On that fateful day, on the sleight of dice provoked by the Palace of Illusions....

Incognito   disguised
Resplendent dazzling
Aeon   An era or yuga
Servitude   Bondage

Musical mysticism

In an alcove of trees was a lake of illusions,
A predicament between life and death.
As the antlers of the stage carried the fire stick of the hapless Brahmin,
He turn to the Pandavas for help,
Pandavas were ignorant of what lied in store for them;
In the predicament of life and death.
Each Pandava spellbound by the aura of lake drunk water turning,
It into last sip of drink and the last pour were lying strewn,
On the Banks of lake till Yudhisthira came to the site to their rescue.
On answering the philosophical questions of the Yaksha,
He was granted life of anyone brother who was lying on the grass.
From the madness of the gambling match, where his wife also was put to stake,
The serene sensibility came over his reasoning and requested for the life of Nakul,
Son of Madri as he was the only surviving son of Kunti.
The need to revive the mighty Bheem or the only,
Omnipotent Arjun was not felt due to cultivated understanding,
And empathy in the journey of life.

Alcove	Recess
Predicament	Dilemma
Hapless	Unfortunate
Strewn	Scattered
Omnipotent	Almighty

Amol Bhagwati

Having abdicated the throne and renounced the world for higher plains,
In the sylvan groves of the Himalayas the Pandavas went on the quest.
To ascend the foothills to the peaks and enter heaven directly in their earthly bodies.
On the path from the foothills to the peaks each of them felt due to,
Some mortal frailty however, on the peaks of Himalayas the celestial chariot.
Had come to the transpose Yudhishthira to the heaven.
Having accumulated merit out of repentance and philosophy,
In the brief spell of reign, being an ideal monarch Yudhishthira could accumulate.
Enough piety to enter heaven in his own earthly body since he struggled,
On the process of conquering himself constantly.

Abdicated	Renounced
Sylvan	Forest
Ascend	Rise
Frailty	Weakness
Celestial	Heavenly
Transpose	Transfer
Piety	Virtue

Musical mysticism

Voluptuous desire fancies and aspirations bring to me relatedness,
A restlessness of purpose intent and intended covert actions.

From a quiver of arrows planted in the vortex of desire and anticipated intent,
A flight of our thoughts and tribulations manifested into a trajectory of purpose.

A volley of arrows swift, soulful and uplifting penetrating the making of mystic,
Upon the balance of benign and blasphemous piercing the eye,
Of the swirling fish of fortune.

Begets a beatific ebullient enigmatic being in the assemblage of voluptuous desires,
To an evolved understanding beyond senses, sensibility and soulful yearning.

Voluptuous	Opulent or shapely
Covert	Secret / Concealed
Quiver	Arrow bag
Vortex	Whirlwind
Benign	Caring
Blasphemous	Offensive or improper
Begets	Causes
Ebullient	Jovial
Assemblage	Accumulation or Gathering
Yearning	Desire or thirst/hunger

Amol Bhagwati

The end who has no beginning and the beginning which does not end:
Love, passion and mysticism which have emblazoned the snow ridden mountains.

The benign aroused meditative energy manifested across aeons.
Music dance and drama caressing the sensibility of nine sentiments.

The temper of the summer and the succour of the rains,
Flashed in his temper and in his benign grace.

The dance of the divine togetherness in the intrepid steps,
Over the astral constellations with Sati in conjugation.

The effulgence of the nascent moon over the fountainhead of renunciation,
The ebullience of dance, verve of drama and meditativeness of music.

Strikes me with benevolence of drinking the dark sinister poison,
That we could partake the nectar of life and beauty in divine grace.

Emblazoned	Inscribed, Adorned		
Benign	Benevolent	**Succour**	Support
Aeons	Eras, Ages, Epochs	**Nascent**	Emerging
Ebullience	Jovial or Cheerful	**Conjugate**	United
Intrepid	Courageous	**Verve**	Vitality or energy

Musical mysticism

What began with a strand of pearls?
Brought an ocean of woes.
To the Sleight of dice, where the stakes,
Would multiply in magnitude.
Corals to diamonds, harnessed horses,
And the elephants battle prone.
The tinkle of anklets and burnished edge,
Of sword of cavalry and infantry.
The city of Indraprastha and the overarching,
Palace of illusions simply changed hands.
Would a quirk of faith bring back luck?
Staking Lady Luck in her magnificence.
Had the dice turned hostile to deceitful caress,
The turn to the Kurukshetra would have many subjugated villains.
The benign mother earth would perhaps be dragged or disrobed,
If Lady Luck would not have been draped by reams of cloth,
By Divine intervention of Dwarka's grace.

Subjugated	Defeated / made powerless
Reams	Layers
Overarching	Primary of Predominant
Benign	Kind
Caress	Tenderness / fond touch
Aeon	A whole era or Yuga
Sleight	Skillful trick or deception
Burnished	Well polished
Quick	Unpredictable act

Entering heaven he was flummoxed,
By the presence of his cousins,
Within the Gods and Indra.
He asked for the where-about of his brother and wife and was taken to,
A grotesque place full of filth, vermin blood and Gore.
He felt the voices of his brothers including Karna and,
Draupadi crying for his presence and good vibes.
He felt ready and eager to stay there forever to provide,
Succour to them this was final test of his forbearance dignity and ability to withstand the odds.
The Pandavas and Draupadi were restored to heaven and,
Yudhisthira joined them after a bath in the celestial Ganga.
The final stage of one conquering through agony,
Ecstasy trials and tribulations and creating a better evolution,
And understanding of the self and the universe within was met by Yudhisthira,
He attained Jaya over himself.

Jaya	Self-victory
Flummoxed	Baffled
Tirades	Outbursts
Filth	Immorality
Vermin	Pests
Gore	Violence
Vibes	Feelings
Succour	Help
Agony	Anguish
Tribulation	Troubles

Musical mysticism

The eye of the whirling fish in the assembly of suitors,
The eye of the fish or earlier that of a bird,
Was within the ambit of eye of the ambidextrous.
The reflection of the fish in the pool of oil.

The balance of the archer and twang of the bow:
The flight of the arrow, blinding the fish:
And oblivious to the expectations of the others.

In a flash brings me to the ill clad sinewy archer,
With a garland of lotuses flowers,
To beckon the new groom, the new vistas of uprising:
And an implicit bonding with the five qualities of an ideal monarch,
Residing in a virtuous brotherhood of the Pandavas:
Righteousness Strength, Agility, Beauty and Wisdom.

Like the life blood flowing within the organs and fins of a fish.
Elements of Air, Water, Fire, Earth and Nether:
Conjugated in a being like elements constituting a body.

Ambidextrous   One who can use both the hands with equal skill
Twang   Pull of bow
Sinewy   strong muscular

Amol Bhagwati

Our Myths are our extended realities,
Characters real or ephemeral extend themselves out of stories,
To create a warp and weft of reality interspersed with imagination.
And fill our beings with agony or ecstasy or both.
Like the arrows of Arjun piercing the fish's eye,
The stories and characters pierce from a very significant intrepid soul.
Like the discourse of Geeta in field of ambivalence our
Intrepid soul ways the significance of our thoughts
And stance where the greater good and lesser evil are again
Intersperse like warp and weft.

Ephemeral	Short-lived
Interspersed	Combined
Ambivalence	Uncertainty
Intrepid	Bold

Beauty

Musical mysticism

The adornment of the frosts in the first quartet of the midnight,
Overflows with the mellowness of the moon,
The sonorous notes are rendered by enchanting beauty.
The imagination starting from the primary note,
Treading on the path of music.
Through the invocation and trebles of Aalap.
The churning of thoughts paused at the deep non-rhythmic gait,
Without the construction of rhythmic music,
Intoxication is ignited, through the journey of amorphous to structured music.
A slight touch of notes in the realms of heart, quite tender and impromptu,
The adornment of the night being the "majesty of night".
Along with the fragrance of the moon,
Creates an aroma which makes the heart and the soul out of bounds.
Through the expansion of the notes the mind is placated,
And the horizons of the moon are expanded.
In the tribute of the swars through the Geetanjali of Malkauns.

Trebles	: Swells
Swars	: Notes of Music
Sonorous	: Resounding
Impromptu	: Unrehearsed
Aalap	: Invocation of Raga
Geetanjali of Malkauns	: Song of joy made of the midnight melody
Amorphous	: Shapeless or Formless

Amol Bhagwati

Water reflecting thoughts reflections and remnants of beauty:
The moonlight sonata plays its symphony in the star-spangled moisture,
Beauty interspersed on the mind expanse and ecstasy proliferates.
Into a nascent form of imagination verse and verve,
Beauty eschews a profound understanding.

Remnants	Leftovers
Sonata	Musical composition
Spangled	Covered with sparkling object
Proliferates	Increase in numbers
Nascent	Budding
Verve	Energy
Eschews	Avoid using

Musical mysticism

Within, infinite myths lie an incense of truth:
Like a whiff pervades in the atmosphere,
Wide spread, fragrant, enveloping and promiscuous.
Like frankincense or a clod of profanity from the perspective,
Viewed, perceived and interpreted.

In the realms of minds, morose or morbid or mellifluous,
In shades of beauty and ribald, profound to prolific,
In the dewy residue, in the stormy waters and never ending litany,
In the turbid thoughts, in timid tribulations and trying trepidations.

Whiff	Smell
Pervades	Suffuses
Profanity	Showing lack of respect for holy things
Promiscuous	Dissolute
Morose	Sad
Morbid	Grim
Mellifluous	Sweet sounding
Ribald	Vulgar
Prolific	Abundant
Dewy	Moist
Litany	A tedious recital
Trepidations	Feeling of fear that something Unpleasant may happen

Amol Bhagwati

In a verse,
Written by the soul,
To the heart,
To encompass and encounter emotions.
Stoic, flagrant, vivacious, inflamed and poised:
As the sixteen digits of the ebullient moon.
It magnificence opulence it's desolation and deprivation.

The soul conjures emotions in deference of the emotions,
Mystic enigmatic bewildering and re calibrating the mind.
In a vortex of thoughts niched and divined,
Like the curse or benediction of music reverie.

Reverie	Chain of thoughts
Ebullient	Full of energy
Deprivation	Disadvantaged
Stoic	Suffering pain without complaining
Vivacious	Full of energy
Opulence	Wealth
Conjures	Creates
Bewildering	Puzzling
Vortex	Mass of air water that pulls things into its center

Musical mysticism

Beauty surpasses understanding,
In the vestment of inner beauty,
Covert eyelids whisper vision beyond,
Beauty is the raiment of the night.

The star studded expanse in the sky,
To sparkle and solitude beyond the soulful,
To muse on the mundane to mystify,
The magnificent munificent and mosaic.

Crimson in the despondent grace,
Snowy white the raiment spoke,
Musical in hues of harmony.
I took my mysterious path,
In the beauty of what we perceive,
Hues and colours take a nuance a step.
Beyond our normal understanding,
In the plethora of our extended space.

Raiment   Clothing
Munificent Bountiful
Mosaic   Medley / variety
Plethora   Excess
Despondent Dejected
Hue   Shade / Colour

Amol Bhagwati

Beauty surpasses understanding or understanding creates mystic beauty,
Fragrant thoughts and benedictions bountiful in their beings.
Proliferate mystic munificent magnanimous in the morose and morbid me.

Benedictions	Blessing
Proliferate	Flourish
Munificent	Bountiful
Magnanimous	Generous
Morose	Depressed
Morbid	Gloomy

Musical mysticism

Beauty juxtaposed against inner calm,
The serenity of the calm sea amidst its' serendipity.
The moonlight penetrating the wavelets of the lotus pond.
Deeply ensconced in the foliage a whisper of love and retribution,
Caresses the wisp of the wings of the soul.
Hovering on the realm of consciousness in the intrepid mysticism of the munificent.

Juxtaposed Contrasted
Ensconced   Entrenched
Wisp   Strand
Realm   Territory
Munificent Bountiful
Hovering   Flying

Amol Bhagwati

Let beauty enthrall me like a sinuous spirit
And intoxicate me like a heady spirit

Filleth my cup to the brim with effusive beauty Sublime,
Eloquent, impassioned beauty

For the sublime in life: Awaken Sensibility,
Bequeathed with a sense of sensitivity

Like a drop of frankincense pristine and fragrant,
Let thy essence pervade to me eloquent.

Like the sound of music poignant and poised,
Yet so vibrant, tempestuous throbbing and composed

Emotions have impregnated me with impotence,
Lead me to thy tavern of everlasting emotions

Let the rivulets of music flow into me from the,
And dwell so, in the final tide consume me.

Let the spirit of beauty pervade into me,
Let the spirit of beauty beautify me and thee.

Tempestuous   Uncontrolled
Tavern   Pub
Frankincense   Fragrant burning incense

Musical mysticism

Paying thousand fold tribute to the feet of Parvati and Parmeshwar
Poetry is a joint ignition of meaning and speech like them.

Perhaps poetry is the thirteenth Swar of music
Or it can be said to be a flood without having rained.

Poetry is like bloomed flower in the season of frost
Sensitivity and subtlety are the roots of poem.

Poetry is the downpour of emotion in the season of summer
Or it can be called the cry of a cuckoo in the days of spring.

Poetry is the culmination of deep and firm vibration
It contains belief in beauty, emotions and the self
Poetry is living proof that the world is not devoid of emotion
When a poet sees a cloud he makes it into a cloud messenger
according to his inclination.

Poetry is the full bloomed moon of literature
Or it can be said to be beauty possessing emotions and sensitivity.
Poetry is a mixed feeling of agony and ecstasy
The feelings of another poet may also bring forth good memories.
The words are Swaras and the poetic meter is the beat
Poetry is the monarch of literature and creativity

Ever poetry is like Ragini emerging from a Raag family
Poetry is mixture of emotion, imagination and logic as a Prayag confluence.

Prayag – Confluences of Ganga, Yamuna and Saraswati.

Amol Bhagwati

Beauty transpires to transcend the boundaries of time.

When the deeds & works of man convert from ephemeral to sublime
The visage of the sun shadows transcends of unhampered scents
When music flows serenely from the beauteous ascents.
Turbid torrential rains pour from the hearts bowers.

Lover blossoms most profound in the spray and midst of heart showers.

The nightingale sings with abandon in a pitched frenzy.

The slumbers of joy, bask in the sunshine of togetherness and fancy
The notes of togetherness play harmoniously to create words of joys.
Where the minds frolic being one and also not one, being known yet coy.

Transpires	Emerges
Visage	Appearance
Coy	Shy

Musical mysticism

What I partake from the cornucopia of nine emotions is from sickle to shield,
From the sweetest ambrosia to the bitterest hemlock.

Seasons ranging from sultry summers to the salubrious spring,
What is well ensconced in the folds of entwined romance?

Froths and boils in the seething heat of anger and turmoil,
When peals of laughter suffuse the froth when an understanding is arrived.

The tempestuous and rabid dark forces which clutter and crowd the mind,
Ultimately at the ascent of moon and descent of sun.
Or otherwise;

A plaintive cry of a peacock in monsoon or the high pitched note of a cuckoo in spring,
The fragrance and hues of flowers blossoming.

A sense of déjà vu of what my mind ravels,
In amazement and wonder......

Cornucopia	Abundance
Entwined	Tangled
Ensconced	Concealed or Hidden
Salubrious	Hygienic or Wholesome
Hemlock	Poison
Cornucopia	Abundance or profusion
Déjà vu	Impression of having seen or experience before
Tempestuous	Stormy or emotional
Suffuse	Pervade or flood
Ambrosia	Nectar

Amol Bhagwati

I see many manifestations of myself,
In the nine sentiments of eros to valour,
From reverie to music in the shades of survival....

Peeping beneath my coverlet of coy demeanor
The sentiment of bewilderment exhilarating ecstasy,
And humour and a tinge of amusement.
Experiencing the experience laid out by the leveller,
Called life in shades of ire wrath and consummated anger.

I live and relive the petals of life in octaves of agony,
Ranging to ecstasy shading from grotesque to beauty.

I see myself thyself and shades in between in season and sentiments.

Manifestation	Appearance
Eros	Passionate Love
Musing	Thoughtful
Peeping	Glancing
Tinge	Touch Exhilarate
Demeanor	Manner or Conduct
Bewilderment	Confusion
Wrath	Anger
Consummated	Completed
Petal	Leaves
Octave	Series of Eight notes
Ecstasy	Joy / Happiness
Grotesque	Outrageous

Music

Musical mysticism

The mellifluous note expanded gently in the forests of the mind,
The beauty of the raga pervaded like the heady scent,
In the environment of the forest.
The fleeting notes and its path created various pathways,
Upon which treaded various aspirations.
Pristine and pure like stream water and bubbling with mirth and joy,
The swift Tanas floated across the untouched water of the Mansarovar.
As the whitened peaks of the mountains clad with snow,
Are embraced by of crown of celestial arches"
Giving mirth and joy to the heart like full fragrant **Malay** winds.
Giving flight to the expanse of the birds' flight,
In the skies and the tribute to the skies.
Through blooms deep rooted solitude and emotions,
Through conjugation blossom thousands of lotuses,
In the proverbial Mansarovar.
The medley of music and tempo conjugate the upper lip of thirst of music.
To drench the amorphous music and meaning.

Mellifluous	: Honey-sweet, soft & rich in flavour or colour or sound
Malay	: Cool pleasant wind from a favourable direction
Amorphous	: Shapeless or formless
Tanas	: Fast glides of many notes of music in a short time.

Amol Bhagwati

Making a note out of word,
Being immersed in the rhythm.
The inner recess of the heart being effusive.
The speech become mellifluous Ragini,
Emotion, rhythm and beauty,
Become three tributaries,
The orchard of the mind become enamoured,
Through the rains of the notes,
Of music and its sprouts,
Is adorned the Ragini of Malhar
With the plumage of peacock.

Through the scented fragrance of the flowers,
Of the heart the mind become joyous,
Treads freely in the orchard of inspiration,

Ragini: Sub raga
Enamoured: Charmed

Musical mysticism

In the realms of mellowness,
Enlightened, satiated, ecstatic,
In the whirlwind of the rhythm of the beats,
Blossomed various lotus or scented flowers.
Transforming into bee I enjoyed the mellowness,
On an extended time in Raag intoxicated eyes.

From note to word and word to note,
The experience expanded and developed.
In a newly grown orchard,
In conjunction with the rhythm of the water bodies.

Ragini: Sub raga
Enamoured: Charmed

Amol Bhagwati

In the intricate inner recesses my heart is ensconced,
With intrepid notes which compose of my being,
My thoughts and my definition.

Into this world ever do morose and unformed,
Ill-informed of intentions and motives of vast worldly expanse.
Few more notes suffuse the chaos ribald and lonesomeness seething within,
A melody rises above the octave pristine poignant and prophetic.

Morose	Sad
Ribald	Vulgar
Seething	Boiling
Octave	8 Notes of music
Pristine	Pure
Poignant	Causing sadness or pity
Prophetic	Far-sighted

Musical mysticism

Within and without understanding and perception,
What has crossed in the figment of imagination and thought;
What tirades what assertions what aspirations what music.
In the discordant chords of thought benign emotions have run blithe.

In temperance, in solitude in reflection in musings,
In nuances of emotions, claustrophobic thoughts and nemesis,
Have raised myself through the music crescendo and ravines.

Figment	Illusion
Tirades	Outbursts
Discordant	Un-harmonious
Assertion	Proclamations
Chords	Harmony
Benign	Kind
Blithe	Happy
Temperance	Sobriety
Solitude	Loneliness
Musings	Reflections
Claustrophobic	Fear of closed spaces
Nemesis	Ruin
Crescendo	Climax
Ravines	Chasms

Amol Bhagwati

After skimming over the basic notes and cavorting with the hallowed atmosphere like in a temple.

The mind welcomes the variegated layers of joy carried by the pure and pristine musical notes and its rendition.

Giving shape form and essence to the unbridled spirits of ecstasy and emotion

The various windows of the mind which are fixed
And transient on the digits of the moon
The second digit of the moon, spreading joy and a fleeting smile
 In the form and shape of sweetness
The lilting melodies of Chandrakauns creates proximity
To the heart with the moon like the Swara of Nishad
The eternal notes of the flutes enlighten the musical atmosphere
And brighten the medley of Swars
Ignite in the heart and soul proximity to
The divine and immemorial and immortal

Unbridled	Uncontrolled
Medley	Mixture
Hallowed	Sacred
Cavorting	Prancing

Musical mysticism

The emotions emerging from the moonlight converted into music
Descended upon the earth through the roof of the sky
Having stayed long on the middle Swara and having cavorted with
Nishad creates unique temperance.

In the orchard and fountains perfumed liveliness makes the eyesight fully fragrance.

On the aspirations which were flowering the manifestation of the mind

Descent in the form of landing birds.

Some vibrations, becoming birds take a flight of ecstasy in the vast lake of imagination.

Certain scented memories after being collected take us to Mansarovar of the mind.

Some doubtful emotions on such occasions increase their cyclic manifestation.

What is soft and harsh has surfaced out and expanded in the lake of sensitivity through various vivacious vibrations.

Amol Bhagwati

The moon's displacement is created by the penetration of the skies through the rays

The pristine and white coolness and its conjugation,
Created brimming love in the realms of the horizons
The heady perfume of the night flowers pervade in the being

The intoxicating and beautiful essence flowing from the balconies of the skies

And the smile creates impatience on the upper lip,
To gain your proximity and nearness
The skies and the being effused with the mellifluence of the Raag of the moon

Even in despair, my beloved the heart effuses a scent of thine in which quartered of night

In the expanding and lilting cadence of the Raag Chandrakauns.

Musical mysticism

Making music out of words
In immersed in the rhythm the inner heart is sanctified by blossoms
into a Ragini.

Emotion poetic meter and beat
Become a threefold river
And the orchards of the mind perfume.

Through the beautiful Swars of music the rain and the sprouts,
The beauteous peacocks pour out the song of Malhar.

Through the flowers of the heart the heady scent,
Makes the mind rejoice and wander

In the orchard of emotions and sweetness as its wind,
Contended rejoices, and its exhilarated.

In the whirlwind of rhythm births many lilies
And scented lotuses becoming a bee I partake its beauty
On an extended time zone in my Raag intoxicated eyes.

Through word music, through music word
The experience expanded and developed
Into a newly blossom orchard.
In consonance of the wavelets of the water body
And its everlasting effects.

Amol Bhagwati

The even song and descending day in soft reverberation and vibration
At the drawing of the day retrieves the scented and perfumed memories,
Night is spreading across the horizon, nascent yet intoxicating
On the pathway of stars, the imagination wanders in the atmosphere's inebriation

The rays of the munificent moon adorn and white the vast horizon
The autumnal moon is resplendent in the skies beauteous and tempestuous

The sheen of love and belongings spreads and immersion into it
The fragrance of the night flowers pervades and allures the mind in commotion

The goblet of wine kisses the upper lip,
What can be more intoxicating than this expansive beauty?
At the full digit of the moon what can be more serenely blissful and awakening?

In the illumination and ascent of the stars, the expansion of the musical notes,
The Ragini amorphous aesthetically and benevolent fills the night skies.

And in the gardens the buds and flowering the light of love,
The fountains emit the beauty of emotions and ecstasy.

Musical mysticism

In the dainty and willful sportiveness of the night,
The beauteous expanse of the moon in the wrap of the night.

The unfettered flight of the bird in the skies' vastness
All these were experienced within the five mystical notes of
Malkauns.

Munificent   Generous
Blissful   Pleasurable
Inebriation   Intoxication

Amol Bhagwati

The flowing of notes into garland or garden of joy,
Beauty flounders in the fragrance of the branching and budding blossoms.
The fountain heads elates emotions of ecstasy,
Suffusing the atmosphere with the cadence of the bowers.
Mystical flowers and fountains transcend,
Into musical mirage and mansions of manifestation.
The strings of the sitar resonate with the echo of:
The sounds of heard, unheard divine sublime and ethereal.
The sway of the beauty leads the mind,
Into realms of space beyond aeons,
Sky and orchards of existence.

Suffusing: Pervading, saturating
Cadence: Rhythm, Beat
Bowers: Groves, Retreats
Aeons: Eras, Ages, Epochs

Nature

Musical mysticism

The deserted corridors of my spatial relatedness, thoughts and emotions resonate
Of desolate desires, suffused souls, ebullient emotions and jubilant joy.
Where I covered my existence into shades of soulfulness of varied hues and shades,
Concurring to my beliefs, aspiration, trials and tribulations all in myriad mysticism.

The oasis which fed and satiated me over various deserts and caravans of life,
In the sands which refine define and confine me as an individual being of difference.
Who has sipped the hallowed waters of serenity, in the opulence of heartstring,
The deserted sands have brought forth in me the virtues of fortitude and plenty.

Spatial	four dimensional
Ebullient	Jovial or cheerful
Myriad	Countless
Heartstring	One's deepest feelings of love or compassion

Acts of omission and commission bring forth to my conscience few questions?

The existence of my being, my actions, reactions, ponderings and dwellings.

Upon the subtle sublime though of what is beyond the realms of understanding.

My subjugated actions, half inclined towards the dilemma and futility of truce or reason.

Is it a treason to my conscience that my heart begins to throb with palpitations of doubts,

The rebuke that dawned upon me in the dregs of my silhouetted thoughts and tirades.

Raising doubts on the inaction as a dilemma between brokered peace and decisive thought.

What I transgressed sullenly in my musings to better understanding and half-baked intent of emotions.

Silhouette	Shadow
Tirades	Outburst
Subtle	Delicate
Subjugate	Overpower
Futility	Ineffectiveness
Treason	Betrayal
Palpitations	Shivers or Tremors
Transgressed	Disobeyed
Sullenly	Angrily / Grimly

Musical mysticism

The twittering of the nascent moon,
The dark spangled Martian shadows.
Cast a mellifluence on the sky-scape,
The drapes of eternal and blooming zephyr,
On the canvas of the night.
Star studded beauty and moisture laden.
Blossoming in the illumination of its expansive vision,
Caressing the vibes of the winds and dormant desires,
In the crystal of rose tinge liquid and rose spangled skies.

Nascent	hopeful, promising
Spangle	glitter, sprinkle
Martian	alien
Zephyr	mild wind
Mellifluence	honey-sweet, soft & rich in flavour Or colour of sound

Amol Bhagwati

The second digit of the moon,
Half expectant, half anticipated,
Emancipated in the dregs of wine,
In the goblet of misery or ecstasy sublime.
Since like a mirage clouded and nascent.
As the first reddened alliteration of dawn
Old emblazoned on the wistful and mystical peaks of yore.

Emancipated   Boundless, Uncontrolled
Nascent   Not mature, incipient
Emblazoned   inscribed, adorned

Musical mysticism

The moon spangled notes reverberate with nascent joy of life,
Beyond the images and mirages veiled.
By the moon in all her dewy tresses.
Like a temple enlighten with the sway,
Of the thousands scented illuminated lamps.
Serene and sombre the night trades gently in,
The illumination of the cadence of Chandrakauns.

Spangled   Sparkling
Nascent   Promising
Cadence   Rhythm
Chandrakauns Primeval midnight, melody.

Amol Bhagwati

The resplendent Rishabh adorned,
By the mellifluous of the evening,
Sways from the cadence of,
The melody in its majesty.
The setting sun rose an aura of foreboding,
Of thoughts from serene to sordid and even morbid.

Through the aspirations of what
Was hope in the distance future?
From the arid situations of today in the quagmire,
Of perplexing perception and confounding thoughts.

Morbid	Gloomy
Arid	Dry
Mellifluous	Beautiful melodies music
Cadence	Rhythm
Sordid	Dark or gloomy
Quagmire	Swamp or marsh
Resplendent	splendid or dazzling

Musical mysticism

The pellucid moon blushed with the tinge of rose-wine.

Unspoken, unexpressed and ambivalent desires half expressed sublime.

The soft silhouettes of canopied shades and the star sprinkled horizon whispers.

Silent words of mystic manifestation expressed in the half-bloomed lotus and lilies.

The blush and bloom so radiant and evoking what unimagined is evident on the expanse of horizon?

The tranquil sublime which transcends beyond the aeons.

And the self of everlasting moonbeams crimson.

Amol Bhagwati

I am carving out my emotions by nail marks on lotus leaf
In the mind Mansarovar emerged thousands of scented lotuses

In each lotus was fragrance of sweet memories
Though avarice and pollution of the atmosphere were interspersed.

The soul becomes a swam crosses snowy mountains to reach
Mansarovar where fulfilled desire, quench the swan and the lake.

The swan stretches its craned neck to look over the snowy realms
Where the feeling of duality is inspired and embraces the heart

For such ecstasy, the soul or the swan always is eager like
 The thirst of Chatak for the moon.

In the twilight the transition of the Komal Rishabh is experience
The moon of the light is also seen like glide in the cloud of the horizon.

When the moon rises clear above the hoziron,
At that time notes of Hanshdhwani emerged and the quest of the swan is fulfilled.

Musical mysticism

On the strings of the Sitar sweet sonorous vibrations of the moon
In the basic note perfumed like a scented lotus
The entire Ragini is pristine from head to toe
The mango pollen being the Madhyam, the cuckoo the Pancham of proud Basant
The king of seasons is in the most aesthetic form of beauty of Raga.

Some unfortunate or arid tree which was devoid
Of the beauteous effect of the season
Were made blessed by the beauty of the Raga
Or the footfall of Dohad and flowered in the hearts.

The fragrance of the Madhukamini became the pathway of the maiden in the night
To search for the beloved on the path of the moon in the illumination   of the stars
In the light of their own joy.

The sonorous and soft Swars of the Sitar are heard
In the orchard and its trees, in the shrill cry of the cuckoo
In the waxing of the moon in the redness of the Kesuda and it scent
In the pathway of the bees
In the love of the beloved and in the mesmerizing of the Cupid.
The vibrations of the Sitar improvise and beautify the moon through Basant Bahar.

Dohad- The rite of a beautiful woman making footfall on a tree which has not blossom to make it blossom with her strength of beauty.

Amol Bhagwati

As the river meanders through the plains,
Spreading prosperity fecundity and a promise of civilisation to dwell.

The banks bring riches to the land inspiration and culture,
Beauty bounty and blossom of each civilisation is,
A mighty river flowing from Aeon to aeon.....

The many dream that float in the minds of empires ....
Like floating lamps of hope and desire jostling between river banks.

Meander　　Wander
Fecundity　　Productiveness
Aeon　　Era
Jostling　　Knocking

Musical mysticism

Purple lilac and violet the shades of luxuriant beauty,
Erupts in the poignant shades of spring.

The dew laden grass verdure of hope and happening,
The crystal blue sapphire of the lakes more beckoning

The mystical gaze of the moon over the overarching willow branches,
Where shadow and light play on each other reflection and reciprocation.

The resplendent moon and the salubrious season manifest in the mind,
Thoughts of ebullient morrow, a comforting arm,
And a heart striving to beautify the mind.

Lilac	Violet
Poignant	Emotional or Upsetting
Verdure	Lushness or Greenery
Overarching	Primary or Predominant
Resplendent	Splendid or Dazzling
Salubrious	Hygienic or Wholesome
Ebullient	Cheerful or Enthusiastic
Beckoning	Signalling or summoning
Sapphire	Indigo coloured precious stone

Amol Bhagwati

In the hallowed woods, where antelopes roam,
Wafts a breeze pristine, salubrious and soothing.
The water of the brooks gently run into its findings,
At either crevice, fall, or a curvet or bending.

Beauty is transient like ether evaporating in the moment,
Like a vestige of the stars path on its astral way.
Moment of togetherness are rare as frankincense:
For an understanding born out of logging and solicitous care.

The litany of voices echo both discord and bonding,
Like the digits of moon over a fortnight fleeting.

Hallowed	Holy or Blessed
Salubrious	Healthy or Wholesome
Crevice	Crack or Split
Transient	Fleeting or Temporary
Litany	Prayers or invocations
Solicitous	Considerate or Attentive
Frankincense	Aromatic gum burnt as incense

Rain

Musical mysticism

As droplets descend from heaven and bring an ethereal whiff
The thoughts of the mind wayward and nomad towards joy drift
The honeyed words of poetry perfume thy existence
Pristine ponderings bring munificent benedictions
Like parched throat eager for a soothing elixir.
The earth scorching the summer eager for blessed distills
The slumber awakened into a beauteous awakening.
The clouds gathering and garnering into mystical beckoning
Droplets turned into streams and torrents culmination
Cleanse the earth and mind for eternal germination.

Amol Bhagwati

In the emotive eyelids of Radha welled an teardrop
That made the waters of Yamuna devout
Some dark deep events descended
 Giving a tribute to the rains!

In the dark vast expansive skies
Radhika is searching for the shapeless Shyam
In deference to the form and being of Shyam
She stayed away from the flute and the peacock feather.

Though it had rained most profusely
The heart and the inner self were arid and dry
The lightning beckons every moment
With Krishna devoid in the heart, where was love in fear?

Radhika was brimming in the heart
And escaped through the welling eyes
The monsoons in Mathura make me impatient and incontinent,
 What thirst also emerged in the eyes of Krishna.

The separation was more bitter than the venoms of Kali
The hearts and beings of Krishna and Radha emaciate
The only union of the souls was in a mirage or a dream
Which was blessed the refreshing showers of rain.

The distance between the souls eloped
When the seven hued rainbows emerged
What a blissful moment to savour....
Alas the slumber of Radhika and Krishna was shattered!

Musical mysticism

The wind is perfumed by the essence of the earth
And season of monsoon is swirling on the whirlwind

The darkness is seen in the day as if replaced by night
The lake is brimming of joy of delighted lotus flower

The being of Chatak bird is satiated from all quarters
The Swati constellation in the droplets of monsoon

The sound of the peacock breaches the basic note and beyond
Of love in the months of Savan and Badho.

The form and formless as if, cloud and rain.
The constellation of Krishna' birth is ominous in Gokul.

River Yamuna is also swelling a joy in the Madhuvan,
The showers of rain perfumed of the moistened earth.

From droplet to droplet and raiment to raiment,
Monsoon is enlivened in Malhar.

Amol Bhagwati

The wind is fragrant with the beauty of earth perfume,
The season of rains is in a whirlwind.
The day seems light the night in the radiant and smiling lilies of the pond,
The heart of the Chatak is satiated completely,
In the raindrops:
Falling in the constellation.
The plaintive note of the peacock pierces and transcends the basic note,
In the moist canopies of Savan & Bhado.
The form and the formless like cloud and rain,
The auspices of the birth of Krishna in Gokul.
The river Yamuna is also swelling in Maduban,
The fall of rain and the scented earth.
From droplet to droplet to torrential rains of Malhar,
The stopping of the cloud on the mount Ramgiri to receive a message.
The fragrance is ominous of imminent rain falling,
The experience of the earth through the showering and fragrant rains.

Chatak   : A bird thirsty for first drop of rain
Ominous : Indicative
Satiated: Quenched
Ramgiri: A mountain in Southern tip of India.

Musical mysticism

The Aalap manifested repeatedly from one layer to another,
Ultimately what is the beginning is perhaps end.
The gait of the melody is deep seated and of immense pride,
The emotive note reflects the ascent and descent of hue of emotions sublime,
Enlightened, blossoms, deep rooted and full of solitude.
Devoid of words, silent, but with eye catching vibrancy.
In the emerald green forests the flicker of joy.
In the vibrancy of the streams and temperance of lakes,
The banks are awe-struck and the hidden unquenched thirst of the sky:
Evident in the darkened clouds
In the backdrop the sky the accented Nishad in the moon,
Breaths of ornamentation and adornment of the basic note.
In the tempo of Shravan in form of rains,
Enlightens and blossoms the monsoons.

Nishad: The note of ni, last note of the octave
Aalap: Invocation of Rag

Amol Bhagwati

Making music out of words,
Being immersed in rhythm,
Emanating from the inner-most recesses of the heart.
The emotions, meter and experience,
Merged has a confluence of three streams,
The orchard of the mind become ignited,
Through the notes of melody,
Through the cadence of rain,
The expanse of Malhar is adorned by the gait of the peacock,
Through the heady fragrance of heartfelt blooms..
The clouded mind becomes unfettered and roams,
In the ripples of the orchard's lake.
Wafted by the moonbeams of mellowness,
Exhilarated, enlightened and ensconced,
In the wavelets of rhythm.
Expanded various fragrant lotus flowers,
The mind transforming into a bee drinks the ambrosia of the experience,
Over the extended time span of the mellifluous melody in its eyes.
From music to word, from word to music the experience,
Expanded and flowered into a newly blossoming orchard.
In the concurrent vibrations of the water expanse.

Cadence: rhythm
Ambrosia: Food of the gods
Mellifluous: pleasant

Musical mysticism

The dark swirling clouds embrace the dark peaks of the mountains
The dark ring roars at that ominous time creating an atmosphere

The beats of the adorned Malhar reciprocate the falling of the raindrops
The atmosphere is entirely cool and pleasing as well as joyous.

The beat is announced by overpowering fragrance of the earth which adorns
The blue green beautiful earth at the occasion of rainfall and the descent of fortune
The high peaks of mountain cover with fleecy white clouds of love
The blue green smile pervades across the nature

In the dark cloudy rains it appears as if.
The peacock feather of Krishna appears to the blue skies green earth expanse.

Seven notes of music scent the nature with divine music.

Amol Bhagwati

Emotions drip drop by drop or raiment by raiment through the substance of water.
The manifestations of the mind create musical fragrances

On the first day of Ashad
The locks of hair the creepers the foliage are delighted forms of nature
The sonorous sound of the basic note like that of attaining the Infinity.

The consonance in the cry of the peacock
The falling of rain is the beauty of nature and the immersion of music
The verses of Meghdoot is the tribute of every heart to love

Swar, nad and music everything is created by water
Rains and the deep hued horizons.

Musical mysticism

One day it rain very profusely
The thirst of the thirsty increased near the banks of lakes.

The water creates layer over the dreams
Which brings back the sweet memories again and again
Making a glance on the clouds like Chatak the leaves and the earth attained elixir again

The peacocks and pea-hens perform their act by song and dance
 The rains rained the entire night
By the joy of Alaap unfettered love was created
The moon eloped in the clouds of the night surrounded by emotions

The soul is drenched by unparallel love
The rains wash the feet of lord / eternal by elixir

It rained prolifically with thunder and claps
In the threshold and exterior, the ecstasy which expanded was limitless.

Amol Bhagwati

The dark deep blue and vast clouds descent constructed emotions are prevented and averted

As if the dark skies and its expanse is with all pervading in the wishes and the aspirations of the mind struggle and collided

With each other and with the self in the commotion of the monsoon What it beautiful and ungainly fought with each other like the contrasting black & yellow clouds.

Bellowed and collided at the whirl of doubtful and debilitating emotions. The heavens began to pour but the sky is aggrieved it is inevitable to the resolve the quandary for the blessings of the rain.

The plaintive note of the peacock pierces the sky like an arrow of music and cloudbursts while something is resolved in the mind.

From lotus eye of Radhika well tear as if the first droplet of rain fell on a lotus leaf.
In the beauteous gait of Malhar struck of higher octave of Malhar.

Crossing the boundaries of peacock plaintive voice reached the skies and constellations.

Torrential rains and stimulates started pouring with the tempestuous tanas.

Tana – Fast movements in music

Musical mysticism

The monsoon creates a beautiful rhythm of water in the memorable month of Ashad.

And water takes form everywhere of the formless refreshes the mind and soul
The drops of water create various vibrations and manifest into emotions
In the expanded space of mind, one thought floats above everyone

In the growth in the water of lilies, in the midday in conjunction with the clouds
One perfumed aspiration of the mind goes on trail who like bee in quest of flower

The beloved locks of hair are expectant the rhythm if stretched prolonged or steady,
In anticipation on beloved moments of arrival.

Where words are Krishna and notes are Radhika and the cloud and lightening are the verses of poetry of the epic Megh Malhar.

www.ingramcontent.com/pod-product-compliance
Lightning Source LLC
LaVergne TN
LVHW041632070526
838199LV00052B/3326